BECOMING KAXAN

STORY BY
Olga Vilkotskaya

ILLUSTRATIONS BY
Sheila Chen

TREATY OAK PUBLISHERS

D1307083

Publisher's Note

Printed and published in the United States of America

ISBN-978-1-943658-98-5

Available from Amazon

TREATY OAK PUBLISHERS

www.treatyoakpublishers.com

DEDICATION

This book is dedicated to Edward Flores, my human dad, best friend, and the person who truly changed my life by teaching me things I never knew about how to behave. But, most important, for his spending countless hours training me to become a certified therapy dog, then always being by my side everywhere I go.

It is also dedicated to Gwen, Miley, and Elphie, my "sisters" who put up with me as I settled in to my new life.

Also, I want to dedicate this book to all dogs (and cats) still looking for their forever homes.

I love Austin, but summers are RUFF.
My fur feels like one giant hairball.

It's Jim Spencer on KXAN!
Time for the weather report.

"The high today will be 105°, folks.
Please stay hydrated and safe out there!"

I just have to make it until evening
when it cools down.

A few well-groomed dogs walk by.
I overhear them talking about me.

"What is that. . . wet dog smell?"
the husky says.

"Ick!" Her friend says. "He
probably lives in the backyard."

"How horrid!"

The third dog stands up to
the husky. "And how do you
think you smell after a
swim?"

"I don't swim!" The husky
shoots back. "That lake has
snapping turtles."

The sweetest sound interrupts their yabbering...

an airborne frisbee!

A crowd of dogs cheers me on.

"What an impressive catch! But where's his owner?"

"He doesn't have one, does he?"

WHOA!

Where can I wait out this storm?

The public library has that big awning... but if the rain comes down at an angle, it won't help much.

Maybe I can hide out at Jo's again. The free dog biscuits are so tasty! But I don't want to overstay my welcome.

This is definitely my unlucky week.

How about that big plastic tent at Radio Coffee? It's a long way to walk, but what I would give for a taste of brisket from that food truck!

Wait, I know! I'll go to Patrizi's and stay under the big tin roof. The black cat lives there, but maybe I can offer to be his butler for a month again.

I feel the air cooling down and ruffling my fur.

There's no time to lose!

A man opens the door and warm yellow light spills onto the concrete.

He brings another man with him.

"Hey, Jim," he says. "Come take a look at this!"

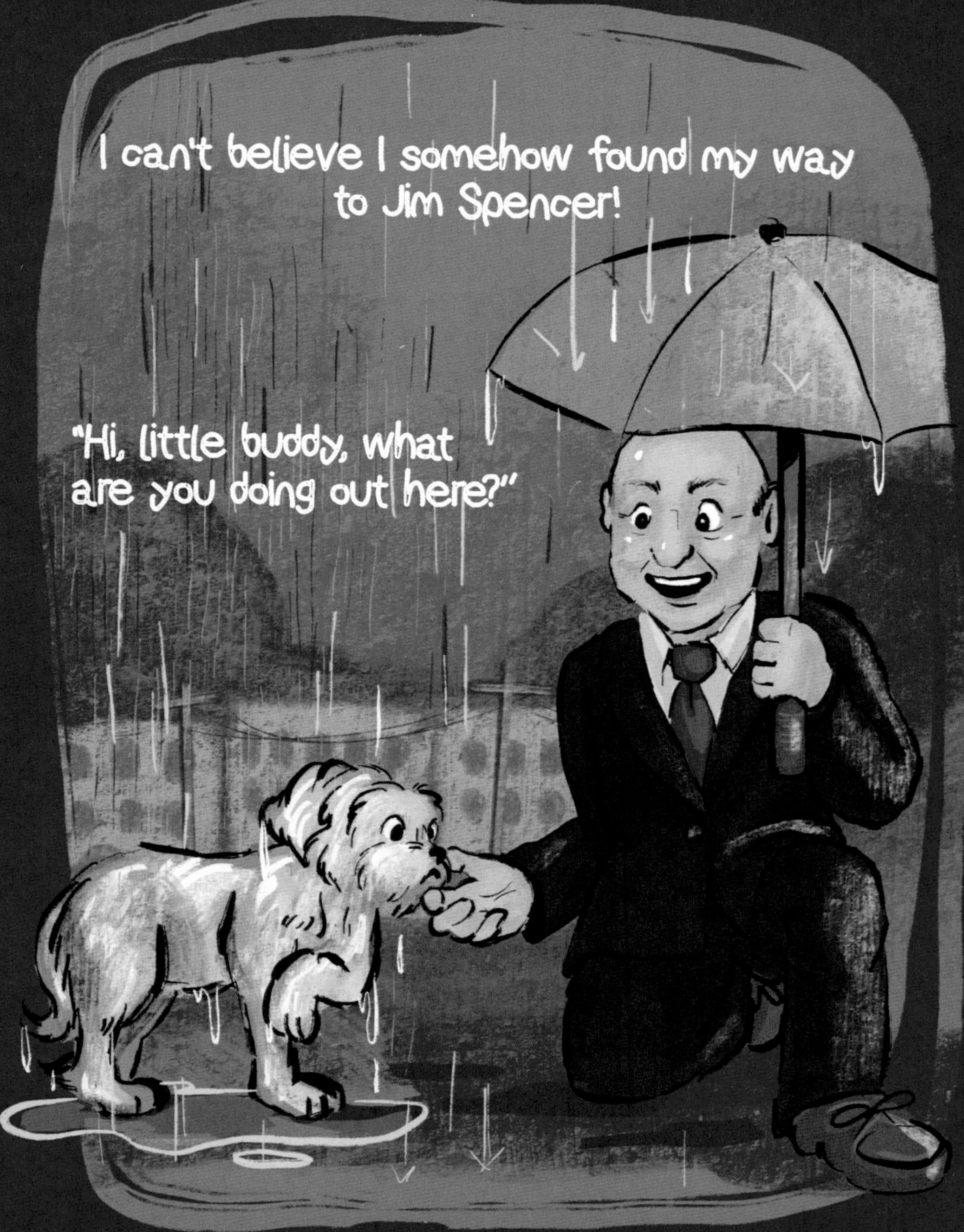

I'd usually run away,
but something about him makes me calm.

All of a sudden, I'm surrounded by TV people.

One lady notices I don't have a collar. "I wonder if he's microchipped?"

"He's so friendly!" says another. "Can he be our KXAN station dog?"

"What if we called him Kaxan?"

Jim smiles at the idea, but looks concerned. "We need to try to find his owners. What if someone is looking for him?"

Then everyone wonders where I could safely stay tonight.

The truth is,
my owners didn't want me.

"Edward," Jim says over the phone. "What do you think about a house guest?"

"What kind of house guest?"

When I step into their home, it feels like the beginning of a new life. I try my best to contain my excitement. It isn't permanent, after all.

"Hi, I'm Gwen. Where did you come from?"

"It's a pretty long story," I tell them.

"You can use my blanket tonight if you like," Gwen says.

"I love stories! I'm Elphie, by the way."

I've never been shown such
unconditional kindness before.
Jim and Edward's family is so welcoming.

That night, snuggled up in Gwen's magic blanket,
I watch the rest of the storm from inside.

I go on.

"The cat ran up to me at the speed of light. Before I knew it, he'd taken his first swipe . . . I thought he'd blinded me!"

"They show no mercy," says Gwen.

"I shook it off. I gathered my strength, and I gave him my biggest . . ."

RAWR!

"AAAGHH!"

Edward emerges from the other room with sleep in his eyes. "Would y'all please keep it down out here?"

I wonder . . .

Would Edward and Jim ever keep a street dog like me?

First thing the next morning,

Edward gives me a bubble bath.

I guess I was a little stinky . . .

Then he wants to show me a trick Gwen and Elphie have been working on.

"Okay, girls," Edward says, "roll over."

"Wow, buddy, great job!"

Elphie looks puzzled. "Wait, that's what Edward has been wanting us to do this whole time?"

Gwen chimes in. "And here I thought he wanted us to read his mind."

"It's no big deal," I say with a shrug. "I've seen this trick a million times at the park!"

Over dinner, Edward and Jim decide they want me to stay with them for good. Edward even suggests that I could be a great therapy dog.

Gwen raises her glass with a big smile. "We'd like to formally welcome you to the family, Kaxan."

I'm overwhelmed with joy.

"Someone pinch me!" I say.

Elphie laughs. "I can pinch you, no problem."

My life changes in the blink of an eye.
Edward is an amazing teacher.
Every part of me is dog-tired at the end of the day . . .
my back, my paws, and especially my brain!

But I love every moment.
I'm growing into a stronger version of myself.

I think everyone needs a little help sometimes.

Each day brings new surprises.

Edward calls me from the other room. "Kaxan! We have someone who needs you. Come quick!"

"Who is it?"

"Jim!"

"Jim? What could it be?"

"Folks, we've got a very special guest with us today."

"I'd like to introduce you to
our new official station mascot, Kaxan!
Boy, do we have big plans for you!"

BECOMING KAXAN

is based on a true story. Kaxan was discovered in the alley behind KXAN-TV in Austin, Texas. He became the station's official mascot and a certified Divine Canines therapy dog.

As part of his work, he visits injured Fort Hood soldiers, patients at hospitals, kids with special needs, and seniors at assisted living homes.

He remains KXAN's spokesdog and continues his great work today, appearing at many animal welfare and rescue events and helping raise thousands of dollars every year for non-profit organizations in the Austin community.

Learn more about Kaxan and his latest adventures at
becomingkaxan.com

RADIO C

AUSTIN
★ TEXAS ★

PATRIZI'S

CAPITOL

LIBRARY

AUDITORIUM SHORES

CONGRESS AVE BRIDGE

JO'S COFFEE

MUD PUPPIES

Olga Vilkotskaya writes poems and stories in Austin. She and her husband have two handsome chocolate labradors, Dante and Virgil, as well as a mischievous cat named Lev. The pack loves to cook bolognese and go swimming (except Lev, who prefers to hunt).

You can find her @olgalindenland.

Sheila Chen @sheilachenart paints dogs and cats for a living! After traveling around the United States as a military family, Sheila and her pack of two dog rescues (Hef and Sierra), son, and husband have decided to grow roots in San Diego.

Sheila is known to travel and do pop ups, so keep your ears alert for pet portraits coming near you!

Want to help a homeless animal?

Here's how YOU can get involved:

ADOPT from a shelter instead of purchasing a pet.
VOLUNTEER at a shelter or help at a pet adoption event.
SPAY OR NEUTER YOUR PET means fewer
fur babies that need homes.
DONATE to your local animal shelter or a national
animal-advocacy group, such as:

American Society for the Prevention of Cruelty to Animals
(aspca.org)

The Humane Society
(humanesociety.org)

Extend a helpful paw
so all our animal friends can find *forever homes!*

with thanks from
Kaxan

Acknowledgments

This book would not have been possible without the vision and talents of:

Christina Lublin
Yvetta Limon
Olga Vilkotskaya
Sheila Chen
Cynthia Stone

Special thanks to:

KXAN-TV
Austin City Limits
Jo's Coffee
Radio Coffee
Patrizi's
Broken Spoke

About Jim Spencer

Jim Spencer is a four-time Emmy Award-winning Senior Forecaster at KXAN-TV, and the longest serving television weathercaster in Austin TV history.

After 30 years of leading the weather team, he chose semi-retirement in 2021. Jim's love of dogs and animal welface causes inspired him to join with his partner Edward in the 2008 purchase of Mud Puppies, an award-winning pet services business in Austin.

You might just see Kaxan greeting customers in one of their three locations or on TV with Jim to promote animal welfare events.

Jim's résumé is a long one when it comes to volunteering and supporting Austin-area charitable organizations of all kinds.

About Edward Flores

Edward Flores has a lifelong passion for dogs, which led to his career change from banking to doggie daycare. When he became an owner of Mud Puppies, he focused on boarding, grooming, and training. Edward is a board member of Austin Dog Rescue, serving as a foster parent since 2009.

Because of Edward's and Mud Puppies' commitment to saving animals from kill shelters, more than 100 dogs have found forever homes. Edward has served on numerous boards in Austin's animal welfare community, including the City of Austin's Animal Advisory Commission.

Edward is also Kaxan's trainer and handler at public events, not to mention his favorite human.

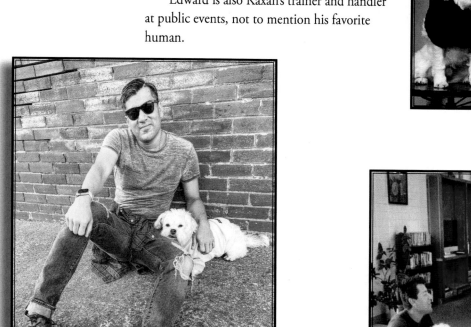